AN UNFORGETTABLE *Date*

SEPTEMBER 19TH

ADNAN HUSSAIN

BookVenture Publishing LLC
1000 Country Lane Ste 300
Ishpeming MI 49849
www.bookventure.com
Hotline: 1(877) 276-9751
Fax: 1(877) 864-1686

Ordering Information:
Quantity sales. Special discounts are available on quantity purchases by corporations, associations, and others. For details, contact the publisher at the address above.

Printed in the United States of America.

Library of Congress Control Number		2019931452
ISBN-13:	Softcover	978-1-64348-659-8
	Pdf	978-1-64348-660-4
	ePub	978-1-64348-661-1
	Kindle	978-1-64348-662-8

Rev. date: 01/08/2019

CONTENTS

An Unforgettable Date: September 19th

An unforgettable date is a book about two males that were different from one another, an affectionate relation that takes over everything.

Being from Islam, to be able to confess your love and relation for the same sex is difficult, but not impossible. People believe Islam is homophobic and doesn't accept this minority in the religion. It's not one act that defines you; it's what your intentions are. Many people have struggled. While people often have such feelings, it's hard for them to confess what they feel for the opposite person. The story defines the unconditional love of the two lovers and how complications are implemented from the first meet. Here it's not two lives that were impacted but three. The men met through social media, but Adam fell for Cameron right from the moment they had met. Read the book to discover the unfolding rollercoaster of an unforgettable date: September 19th.

To my wonderful readers:

In every relationship, there are arguments, fights, laughter, crying, and many ups and downs. There is stuff said in anger, crazy exes, attitude problems, and jealousy. But at the end of the day, if you truly love someone, you will be around through the good and the bad.

CHAPTER 1

The Meet

It was the evening of September 19th, Adam was sitting in his car outside the shopping mall, waiting for his family while they were shopping. Adam was browsing the net when he came across a profile and decided to have a conversation. This unknown faceless profile was frustrating Adam as there was no image of who this individual was. A "*Hello*" turned into exchanging face pictures with a meet that same very night. Before they had met, the blank profile was adamant on having Adam's number, but "*No*" was the answer. After talking for a while, a name was revealed from the blank profile stating, "*I am Cameron.*" Both said they want to meet in an hour at the subway.

Adam was a guy who never did anything like this. Cameron had a previous relationship with a man.

When Adam arrived at the subway and saw Cameron (the faceless profile on Grindr), they both were captivated. Both the men named the subway as the first location. Cameron called Adam in to his car, and they both went for a drive. During this car ride, Adam started the conversation with a "*Hi.*" He looked at him with a smile on his face. "*Hey,*" said Cameron. Like this, the conversation of "*Where are you from?*" and "*How was your day today?*" got started. As the drive was going, they both stopped in an unknown car park and turned the engine off. Adam was in the passenger seat, with Cameron repositioning his body to face Adam. Cameron placed his hand on Adam's thigh. Moments later, both gradually started moving in closer, closer, and closer. Adam's lips were touching Camerons's, but there was no movement. The pair was nervous; it was intense, it was something that Adam had never done before. The car windows were all steamed up, lights were off , and it was quiet. No one spoke, only felt, and they exchanged the first kiss on this unforgettable date. The pair got so engrossed with each other that they didn't even realize the time, how it became past midnight from evening. After four long hours of deep kissing, the pair got a milkshake and, in the end, Adam exchanged his numbers with Cameron. It was all new for Adam. He felt so different, so happy and attached.

Adam was so restless to meet Cameron again. He could not sleep and was just twirling around in his bed, thinking about Cameron and the question asked by him. *Will you meet me again tomorrow?*

The morning after was a new start for Adam. He was completing the final year of his bachelor's degree at university. He woke up thinking of what his day at university will be like. Not long after, though, he received a "good morning" text from Cameron. It bought a big smile to Adam's face. Without further ado, a reply was sent back and in the same way. Text messages were being exchanged all morning. Both Adam and Cameron were not paying attention to what they were doing but texting each other all morning.

During the exchange of texts, Adam told everything about his life and past. He stated, "*His family is planning for him to get married and settle down.*" He opened up and said, "*I am bisexual, and I have a fiancée.*" Cameron made a statement that really hurt Adam's feelings. He said, "*Does she not fulfill your sexual desires?*" This made Adam upset and no reply was sent.

Not long later, Cameron called Adam and said, "*Can I meet you this evening?*"

Adam replied, "*Is there anything else left to say?*"

Cameron explained, "7 *p.m., first location,*" and hung up.

Adam was upset with what Cameron had said, but at the same time excited to be meeting at 7 p.m, as he just really liked him.

A few hours later, Adam reached the first location on time; however, Cameron was nowhere to be seen. He waited fifteen minutes, yet no one was there. Thirty minutes passed by. Still, no one was there yet. It got to 9 p.m, and Adam received a text from Cameron saying, "*I'm sorry, I will be there in fifteen minutes.*"

Adam said okay and carried on waiting.

Upon Cameron's arrival, Adam again went into Cameron's car and went to the quiet car park, which they both named the second location. The original plan was for an intimate encounter, but ended up being deeper than that.

Cameron: "*Do you want to make this a regular thing?*"

Adam: "*Are you asking me out?*"

Cameron: "*Yes.*"

Adam: "*I really liked you from the time I met you, but I have never done anything like this before. I've never been in a relationship with a guy before.*"

Cameron: "*I have been in a relationship with a guy, but it's over between us both, and I will meet him tomorrow to give it a verbal ending.*"

Adam: "*Okay.*"

The next day, Adam was at work and was waiting anxiously all day for Cameron's text of how it went between him and his ex-boyfriend. He did not receive a reply that day. Then came Friday morning. Adam went to the sexual health clinic for an appointment and coincidentally saw Cameron at the reception. Adam took a seat waiting for his turn when Cameron sat beside him and texted him saying: "*Hi.*"

Adam said, "*What do you want now? Why are you playing with me?*"

Cameron replied, "*Because I like you!*"

Adam said, "*How did yesterday go?*"

Cameron: "*It went well. We got some food together.*"

Adam: "*Glad you enjoyed it.*" (But was feeling really hurt inside.)

Cameron: "*I need to talk to you.*"

Adam: "*Cool, after the appointment.*"

Cameron had finished early and waited for a few minutes, but Adam had gone inside late so was not finished for a long time, and his battery had died. Cameron messaged him saying, "*Meet me at my house tonight at 8 p.m.*" After a few hours, Cameron texted Adam again saying, "*If you're free, come to my house now.*" Adam had a lecture that day but left early so he could meet Cameron. Before going, Adam asked, "*What's your favourite chocolate?*" to Cameron. "*White Lindor,*" said Cameron. Before going to visit him, Adam rushed to the local shop to buy this chocolate; however the first shop he went to didn't have this type of chocolate, so he went to two other shops just to get the white chocolates.

He arrived outside Cameron's house and parked the car. Standing outside Cameron's house with his heart beating, he got goose bumps thinking of what must've happened yesterday between Cameron and his ex-boyfriend. Nervously, he knocked on the door. "*Welcome,*" said Cameron as he opened the door and let Adam in. "*Take a seat,*" he said.

Both sat down on the sofa.

Adam: "*So what happened yesterday?*"

Cameron: "*Nothing much.*"

Adam: "*Between you and your ex-boyfriend?*"

Cameron: "*I'm sorry, but I have loyalties toward him. I've known him for four or five weeks and I can't leave him. I really like you, though.*"

Adam: "*Wow, okay, you said it was finished between you both and you were going to give a verbal end. Like, what happened to that?*"

Cameron: "I'm sorry."

Adam: "*Its fine. I shouldn't have met you. Anyways, these chocolates are for you. Hope you're happy together.*" He smiled and left.

Adam left upset. He went straight to the gym and vented his anger out by working out recklessly. Cameron called Adam and messaged a few times; however, Adam did not respond at all. After a while, Adam realized, he didn't want to upset him and would be okay being friends with Cameron. The pair met on that Friday night and just spoke about family and about their lives. Adam just wanted to be there for Cameron.

The next morning, it was Adam's graduation from a degree he had already completed. He did not enjoy it at all, as he was really upset from what happened the night before. It ruined his whole mood and really hurt him. Adam met one of his best friends, Billy. He told him what had been going off in the past few days and how he had developed these new feelings.

Billy: (Viewing Cameron's picture) "*This guy messaged me also asking to meet up.*"

Adam: "*No way! I can't believe it.*"

Billy: "*Yeah, but I did not reply. I would not trust him if I was you. He does not look like a decent person. He looks more of a player.*"

Adam: "*Come on, man, you can't judge a book by its cover. How can you be so sure he's a player?*"

Billy: "*I can tell. Anyways, do what you feel. Just keep the relationship to a limit as you have a fiancée and you don't want to ruin things with her.*"

Adam: "*I told him everything and he's okay with it.*"

Billy: "*You sure, yeah? I just don't want to see you getting hurt, man.*"

Adam: "*Yeah, he's fine with it. He knows everything about me. I told him all.*"

Adam left for his home after meeting Billy. On the way home, he was just thinking about what Billy had said, but could not stop thinking about Cameron at all.

Adam took Cameron the next day for a late-night McDonald's drive and just spent thirty minutes with him, as Cameron said he had to sleep since he had work in the morning. The pair were to originally meet in the evening as Cameron had promised but didn't turn up, but when he was hungry, he called Adam. In the same way, the couple spent two more days together, meeting and talking as normal friends.

Adam was under the hospital as he was told he was terminally ill with bowel cancer not long before meeting Cameron. He had a procedure the next day, so he asked Cameron if he could pick him up from the hospital as he would be sedated and would need someone to pick him up. Cameron agreed. This was the fourth day they were meeting after Cameron had decided not to officially be with Adam.

It was at the hospital where Cameron went to receive Adam. When he reached there, Adam had been given more drugs then he should've received and was all hyper. Amid all this, Adam spoke out his feelings and said "I love you" to Cameron. Adam under the influence of drugs expressed his true feelings, even though he knew Cameron did not want to be with him. They both went for a meal together and ended the night with a romantic drive. Before going, Cameron said, "I will tell you my answer tomorrow regarding reconsideration of my decision."

It was Friday, over a week since the pair had first met. Again, Adam went to Cameron's house, but this time all prepared to hear another rejection from the guy he dearly loves which is Cameron. The couple sat down in the same way as they did the last time they had met at Cameron's house.

Adam: "So what you decided?"

Cameron: "You love to convey messages through songs, so today I will convey my answer in your style, through a song." Cameron played a song in Arabic, which translates to "My heart is for you, even though I do not know you, by my heart belongs to you!"

Adam, not having a clue, just listened to the song. Suddenly, Cameron jumped up and started kissing Adam. He started making out with Adam.

Cameron: "*I choose you.*"

Adam: "*Why me? Thought you had loyalties to your ex?*"

Cameron: "*I spent the last four days with you and no one has ever loved me like you have. You've put love in my heart, and I want you and only you.*"

Adam: "*Okay, but I'm no second choice. I think you should think again, as I do not want to be hurt.*"

Cameron: "*I have done, and I want you.*"

Cameron had finally realized he had fallen for Adam and wanted to be his official boyfriend. Both made a fresh start and new promises.

Adam had two conditions.

Adam: "*We do not get family involved.*"

Cameron: "*Okay.*"

Adam: "*We both see each other when it's convenient for the other.*"

Cameron: "*That's fine. I have two conditions also.*"

Adam: "*What are they?*"

Cameron: "*No more apps to meet other people?*"

Adam: "*Done. I've not been active on that since we met.*

Cameron: "*Don't ever lie. We always tell the truth, as I've been cheated on by my ex-boyfriend and don't want to be cheated on again.*"

Adam: "*I won't. And I hope you don't cheat on me; however, I trust you as I know you wouldn't do anything like this.*"

And like this, Adam only spent four days with Cameron and Cameron fell for Adam. This new relationship was official but kept hidden from everyone, except from Adam's close gay friends. Cameron never even told his friends. He kept it hidden from everyone but was happy on starting a new relationship together.

This is when Adam should have clocked on that Cameron was not being entirely truthful and should have ended it here, however Adam's mistake only was that he was deep in love.

CHAPTER 2

Finally Official

After becoming official, the pair would meet every day. Adam gave all his time to Cameron, spending hours with him. Adam would go to university from 9–5 p.m., and Cameron would work until 5 p.m. also. The pair used to meet at the first location at 5 p.m. and spend evenings together till 11 p.m. at the very earliest. When the couple got together, Cameron had made a promise, he would be visiting London only one weekend a month, but was visiting every week, even though his family relationship was not strong. A week after becoming official, Adam had to go on a family holiday as his cousin was getting married abroad. He had told Cameron about the wedding since the time they had met. Adam left for the holiday, spent two weeks abroad, and had come back. Adam landed, and as usual, Cameron was late. Adam waited for over thirty minutes until he saw Cameron, and they both headed to the car park. It was a romantic evening; the sky was clear, with fog in the air. The car was parked on the top floor. Cameron and Adam made their way there. Outside the car, Cameron just grabbed Adam and started making out with him.

Cameron: "*I missed you so much and these lips of yours.*"

Adam: "*I missed you even more and am happy to see you now.*"

Both got in the car, when Cameron received an image from a guy he used to talk to through Grindr. Adam was shocked.

Adam: "*You still have people on you're snapchat that sent you nudes? I thought you had deleted all the guys you used to talk to?*"

Cameron: "*I have done that. I just haven't spoken to this guy for a long time.*"

Adam: "*That doesn't mean you still have him on Snapchat. I deleted everyone ever since I met you and a guy I know from abroad. He likes me, but I didn't have sex with him.*"

Cameron: "*You're taking this wrong.*"

Adam: "*I'm not. I finished it with everyone, because I love you. I could've slept with the guy abroad, as it's only been a few weeks since we've been official; however, I never cheat, I had promised you.*"

Cameron: "*I'm sorry. I'll block him now.*"

Adam was upset, but just put a fake smile on his face. They left for Cameron's place. They spent the night there; however, after the pair had a shower and just laid together, Cameron noticed something on Adam's leg.

Cameron: "*What's this?*"

Adam: "*I don't know.*"

Cameron: "*I think its pubic lice.*"

Adam: "*Oh no! What do I do now?*"

Cameron: (Picking up a tweezer) "*Don't worry, I will handpick them all it, and we will get cream in the morning.*"

Adam: (Amazed by him) "*Thanks so much, I appreciate it.*"

Cameron: (Picking out the pubic lice from Adam's legs) "*Don't worry. It may not be from you, it could be from me also, you never know.*"

(Adam, checking Cameron's body, found some pubic lice).

Adam: "*Hey, I found some, give me the tweezer, I'll take yours out.*"

Adam and Cameron cleaned each other up and slept together. During the night, Adam got ill and required medical but Cameron just laughed it off and didn't see how much difficulty Adam was in. *Where was all the promises Cameron had made saying he'll be supportive.* Not long after, Adam forced himself to sleep and soon after it was sunrise. The local shops had opened. The pair bought some pubic lice cream and rubbed it on each other's body. Adam left for his house, saying goodbye to Cameron and thanking him for what he did. The couple left the cream on for over twenty-four hours and didn't meet until the effect of the cream had worn off.

A couple of days later, Adam sent a text message to Cameron asking to meet up urgently. After Cameron had finished work, the couple met at the hospital as Cameron had been coughing for a few weeks and just wanted to make sure everything was okay. Cameron blamed Adam, stating it was his fault he had been coughing. Due to Adam's illness, Cameron blamed him continuously; however, it was nothing connected to him. It was a chest infection. Adam was really worried for him. Nevertheless, Adam was there with him all night in the hospital throughout every test. Adam did not leave Cameron alone at all, except for when it was dawn and Adam went to pray to god.

Adam bowed down to his lord in the morning prayer known as *fajr* and raised his hands to pray to god for Cameron's results to be normal. While in the hospital, Adam surprised Cameron with two tickets to Ireland he had booked.

Adam: "*I want to take you to Ireland.*"

Cameron: "*Really? When do we go?*"

Adam: "*Next weekend. I booked a weekend for you as I know you have work during the week.*"

Cameron: "*Yeah. We'll have fun.*"

Adam: "*But you're driving to the airport, and I haven't booked the hotel, so you book it and just send me the bill.*"

Cameron: "*Cool, I'll drive and book the hotel once we are done here. There was this guy I used to do a fashion show with, he also had asked me to go with him to Ireland.*" "*I think he's gay, and likes me.*"

Adam: "*Oh ok.*" (Feeling really terrible by what had just been said)

All the tests were complete. Cameron was fit to go home as he had got the clear from the doctors that he is fine. Cameron's samples were taken and sent to the lab to be grown for a more specific result after he insisted that he was ill and had caught something from Adam.

CHAPTER 3

First Date in London

After the hospital discharge on the very same day, the couple went to London. However, Cameron wanted to go to the GP before he went anywhere. Even though he was discharged from the hospital, he was not content. Adam spent the night with him in the hospital and they were on the way home.

Cameron: "*I want to go to the GP surgery.*"

Adam: "*Okay! Where's that?*"

Cameron: "*Along the way.*"

They both went to the GP. Adam went with Cameron inside, but Cameron did not want him to go inside with him to see the doctor, so Adam waited in the reception. And of course, it was Cameron's choice whom he wanted to take inside. The doctor gave the clear. Adam dropped Cameron home and went to take some rest after agreeing to meet at 3 p.m. that afternoon.

Adam had packed his bags to go to London and sat waiting. He waited until 5 p.m. until he messaged Cameron if he was still coming. Cameron did not reply for four hours, leaving Adam hanging. Later that day, Cameron called Adam and said "*let's leave now.*" They got there a bit late, but had a nice evening together and explored London the whole night. They visited London Bridge, Westminster Pier, Big Ben, and London Eye. It was 4 a.m. in the morning and the pair were still on their long walk. Cameron showed so many attractions to Adam, he had not seen before.

The pair stayed awake the whole night. Cameron said during the night he had to go for a meeting for an hour, even though this was never disclosed beforehand, and the short trip was for the pair to enjoy. It was to do with a famous fashion show he was a volunteer in. Cameron left at 9 a.m. Adam packed all the bags and was waiting in the lobby from 10 a.m. till 1:30 p.m. Cameron did say one hour but didn't return for a long time. Adam waiting patiently, thinking if this holiday was a business meet or quality time between the two. Adam did not have lunch as he was waiting for Cameron, who had already eaten with the guy from the Fashion week meeting, who seemingly likes him and is gay. With Adam's long-term illness, he must eat at certain times, but the fact he waited for Cameron so they both could eat together was sweet—but Cameron had eaten, knowing Adam is waiting for him. Adam got upset all Cameron did was placate him, not even showing any regret. Adam could never be angry or upset more than five minutes with Cameron.

They both happily, with Adam forgiving what happened had left for their home city after enjoying a nice trip in London.

CHAPTER 4

Ireland

A few days later, Cameron was surfing the net and found some hotels to stay at while in Ireland. He sent some hotel pictures to Adam to view and both gave agreed on a studio apartment. Cameron paid for the hotel; however, Adam did not want him to pay for it all, so he said, "*Send me the total cost and I'll contribute also!*" Even though Adam did not have enough money in his account, he gave less money than he should have. He did not tell Cameron that he did not have enough; he just kept quiet and sent what he could after borrowing some money from his sister, just so Cameron didn't have to pay for the apartment himself, even though Adam had paid for the flights.

On the flight to Ireland, Cameron questioned Adam about the hotel contribution.

Cameron: "*Why did you send a specific amount of money to a decimal figure?*"

Adam: "*I just made a random guess and sent it.*"

Cameron: "*But why such an amount?*"

Adam: "*I'm sorry, it was just a random guess.*"

Cameron knew clearly that Adam was lying. Cameron rebuked Adam for sending such an amount, knowing he is just a student and does not earn that much as he only works part-time. Cameron was a successful Mechanical Engineer earning loads whereas Adam a full-time student.

Cameron: "*This shows what you think of money.*"

Adam: "*Money is nothing for me; I care about people and feelings.*"

Cameron was furious; however, his anger was justified, and Adam knew he should not have sent such an amount. He should've sent more. He felt so guilty. Adam apologised continuously but Cameron did not let it go.

While in Ireland, the couple went to a nightclub. While dancing, Adam's drink got spiked. Adam was acting different. Cameron realized Adam's behavior was different, so he decided they should leave. On the way to the apartment, Adam was demanding a donner kebab as stated by Cameron who had explained everything the next morning to Adam. Cameron got him one. All the way home, Adam was not acting normal and was bucking all sorts. The couple reached back and had food. Cameron was really stressed and was panicking with Adam that nothing happens to him.

The next morning, Cameron asked Adam if he remembered anything and, like in every scenario, no one remembered whether their drink was spiked or not.

Cameron: "*You don't remember anything?*"

Adam: "*No! Why?*"

Cameron: "*You were saying you're going to ask your mum to get us married.*"

Adam: "*No way!*"

Cameron: "*Yeah! And you were expressing how much you love me.*"

Adam: "*I swear I don't remember anything.*"

Cameron: "*Yeah, man, but I found it cute. I did get worried but then checked online and everything seemed okay.*"

Adam: "*Maybe it should happen more often!*"

The couple had a shower together and left for sightseeing. On the flight back home, the pair were talking when Adam asked a question.

Adam: "*So what you doing tomorrow? Shall we meet?*"

Cameron: "*I have other priorities than doing other things.*"

Adam was really hurt by this. He was thinking he was not important in Cameron's life and does not hold any value.

Adam: "*Is everything okay? Have I said anything?*"

Cameron: "*Yeah, everything is fine!*" They got KFC, had sex in the car and drove home.

CHAPTER 5

Lies Caught

It was a Saturday evening. The couple had a date. While on this date, Adam received an image from Billy, who at the time was talking to Cameron's ex-boyfriend. The image was of the conversation where Cameron's ex-boyfriend clearly stated the meeting Cameron and his ex-boyfriend had back in September, where Cameron asked for another chance and he did not end it that day. Upon seeing this, Adam was so upset and felt betrayed. Cameron never said that he asked for another chance; he told Cameron he had "*loyalties*" toward him. Adam felt like he was kept in the dark. After all, he could've just stated the truth. *Did Adam have a clue about this undercover relationship; no!*

Cameron: "*I was scared, we newly got together.*"

Adam: "*Yeah, we newly got together, but you said you wouldn't lie about anything. Well, at least that's what you said on the first night we had met.*"

Cameron: "*Yeah, I know, but I just didn't want to lose you. I thought you won't understand.*"

Adam: "*And what makes you say that? Till now I have listened to everything you have said and always advised you. Why betray me all this time?*"

Cameron: "*I'm sorry.*"

Adam: "*It's not about saying sorry; it's about the principles. Based on honesty, you could've told me.*"

Adam was really tormented by this and did not speak to Cameron. But this is how they both were. If they had an argument, they would be fine within five minutes. Cameron tried to calm Adam, but Adam couldn't stay angry for to long also, and as always made up after calming down. Cameron understood that in all fairness, he should've told Adam. Nevertheless, Cameron got back at Adam by bringing up the history when Adam gave less money that he should have for the apartment in Ireland. Adam felt so ashamed, but so hurt. Adam dropped Cameron off at home. Neither of them had spoken to each other that night. Cameron did not have anything to say in his defence.

Adam went to work at 6 a.m. the next morning and finished in the afternoon. Upon finishing work, Cameron arrived. Both sat in the car and spoke about their differences. Adam forgave Cameron, but Cameron wouldn't forget anything. They both agreed to forget what happened. Who knew this was another game plan by Cameron. *Adam forgave him and the pair we're happy.*

CHAPTER 6

Decision Time

Adam's fiancée was returning from the family holiday they all had gone to a month ago. He went to the airport to receive her. He was upset at how Cameron would take this, but Adam never hid anything from Cameron, even though it never was the same from the other side. Both the men met up and Cameron took a decision to limit their meet. Adam started crying. He didn't want to lessen anything to do with Cameron. He truly loves Cameron.

Adam: "*We will still meet the same times we used to meet.*"

Cameron: "*Nope, you will be busy, and I don't want to disturb.*"

Adam: "*Am I ever busy when it comes to you.*"

Cameron: "*I know but...*"

Adam: "*No ifs or buts. We will meet the same way we used to.*"

And they both agreed to keep everything the same and not to change anything, even though Adam's fiancée Layla had come back to the country. In the same way, the pair would meet and spend the same amount of time with each other.

Weeks passed by, Cameron was working, and Adam gave time to both Cameron and Layla, working part-time and studying full-time. Being so busy, Adam did not sacrifice spending time with Cameron.

Many times, Adam had to ask Cameron for time as Cameron would say he's busy. It came to this much that Adam had to meet Cameron by saying he needed help in his studies, just to spend time with him. Cameron knew everything, but deliberately would torment Adam and play with his emotions.

A company approached Adam after viewing his profi le online. They said Adam could be eligible for the scholarship and invited him to London for an interview. However, Adam did not want to go without Cameron, so he messaged Cameron asking if he should go ahead with this opportunity. And Cameron would never reply to Adam in time, as he always wanted Adam to wait. Adam could not exceed his waiting time for more than one hour. Adam booked a bus ticket as he did not get a response, and upon booking his bus ticket, he received a call from Cameron asking "*if everything was okay?*" Adam explained everything and told him how he did not reply in time, and he didn't want to lose this opportunity, so he booked a bus. Cameron was really angry due to this so the pair travelled to London in Cameron's car, despite booking the bus. Upon reaching there, Adam was being escorted to the interview room, and Cameron decided to start flirting with the receptionist and give him his Instagram ID. The receptionist had already spoken to Adam about life and who he has travelled with today. Spencer, the receptionist, went and told Adam how his boyfriend was flirting with him while he was attending the interview. Cameron tried to cover it up by telling Adam he had blocked him and there was nothing happening. It was just a normal add, even though he knew the receptionist was gay and asked Cameron if he was single. This just ruined the whole mood of the day, and Adam believed Cameron and let it go, based on the trust between them. This was happening regularly, but Adam was not paying heed to the signs of the cheating he was receiving by Cameron.

On a positive note, Adam got a three-year scholarship, and gave Cameron a treat.

CHAPTER 7

The Hospital Visit

Life is unpredictable. It is too short to distinguish how long we are to live. It should be enjoyed. Who knew after getting some good news of getting the scholarship, Adam would get some news that would change his life forever?

One bad habit of Adam's was whenever he would be in pain, he would not tell anyone. He did not want to get anyone worried, as in the past Cameron had mocked his illness and left him to be in pain.

It was a normal day, like every other day. Adam had gone to university as a daily activity, but this day was different from all. Adam started getting pains in his stomach; he was vomiting. Sweat was dripping from his forehead. He gasped for air, could not even take a few steps. *What was going on? No one had an idea!* Adam had to be rushed to the hospital.

The doctors checked Adam and gave a verdict: "*This is a case we have never seen before.*" Adam was told he was terminal and that he would never recover. He was told he needs urgent care and needs to tell his family members. Adam was stubborn and did not want to tell anyone. He did not want anyone knowing the severity of his illness as it would get everyone stressed out. Adam's sister and uncle came to visit.

They came inside and sat beside the bed.

Adam's uncle: "*What's going on?*"

Adam: "*Nothing, just a normal check up.*"

Adam's uncle: "*Then why are they keeping you in?*"

Adam: "*They want to do further tests.*"

Adam's sister: "*You lied to us the last time also. You said it was a normal check up, but you ended up staying two weeks. After all, what is wrong? Please tell us.*"

Adam: "*I'm fine. Don't worry!*"

A while later, as Adam's uncle and sister were leaving, they encountered Cameron. Adam's uncle greeted Cameron and left.

Adam: "*How did you know I was here?*"

Cameron: "*Because I'm a Mechanical Engineer and I can track you down.*"

Adam: (Shocked) "*Ok! Can I ask you a question?*"

Cameron: "*Yeah!*"

Adam: "*When I die, after how long will you move on? And when I die, how will you know I'm dead?*"

Cameron: "*Firstly, you're not leaving me. I won't move on because I love you! And I will check the local death registrar.*"

Adam: "*Nice! You got a full plan to track me down if I die. Haha!*"

In the same way, the couple were talking. No one realized when visiting house were over. It was getting late; Cameron had to leave as he had to go to work the very next morning.

Whilst in hospital, the pair would meet every day. Cameron knew Adam's favorite was chocolate, so he would always bring chocolate when he would visit. The pair did not spare the hospital with their romance. They started in the room, as Adam had his own room, regarding it as a suite!

Adam did not let his long-term illness get in the way of his life. He would write his dissertation in the hospital by staying awake till 3 a.m. and would speak to tutors via Skype. The tutors were impressed, looking at the dedication of Adam to his course. Not soon after, Adam discharged himself, so he could enjoy the perks of life outside in the world and not in the hospital room. Though Adam had been discharged, Cameron did not recover fully from his chest infection, which he regarded to be HIV at this point. He indirectly accused Adam of transmitting him with HIV and said to Adam he should get checked out by the sexual health clinic. Adam went manic.

Adam: "*I've not slept with anyone in the past three months except for you, and before our relationship started, we both had got tested. Yeah, I admit I may have had sexual transmitted infections in the past, but that doesn't mean I have HIV.*"

Cameron: "*I'm worried I may have caught something.*"

Adam: "*How could you catch something when you've only slept with me? And if I'm clear, which I'm telling you I am, then it means you've been sleeping around and may have caught it from someone else.*"

Cameron: "*I've not slept with anyone, but let's just get checked.*"

The couple went separately to get checked. Everything was negative. This was another trial by Cameron. No one had any kind of disease. Cameron was getting worried for nothing. Adam was hurt deeply by this accusation, and the pair didn't talk.

CHAPTER 8

Birthday Weekend

It was near the end of the year; Adam's birthday was approaching. Adam spent a day with his fiancée. Layla took him to Manchester and planned a surprise party for him there. Adam enjoyed a lot with his family at the party. It was a great reunion as he had not spent time at all with his mum and family ever since he had met Cameron did not have to worry as he lived alone, away from his family.

For Adam's birthday, both men had decided to go to London. Cameron booked everything to have a great weekend, but who knew this weekend was going to be a disaster? As planned, Adam arrived at Cameron's workplace and from there they drove to London.

The next few months were critical. Such things happened that changed not two but three people's lives.

CHAPTER 9

First Break Up

London calling again. During the festival season, the city is full of life, lights, and lust. The pair wanted some time alone, where they could be away from worldly affairs—just the two of them.

The Continental Hotel in London was booked and upon arrival the pair was greeted and shown their romantic room. The pair romanced like never and ordered a takeout. Whilst time was ticking away, it was minutes before Adam's birthday when Cameron set a surprise on the bed, and at twelve midnight, he made Adam open his eyes and see this amazing effort of his! Adam was spellbound. He hugged Cameron and thanked him. The pair laid on the bed that had been beautifully decorated with slow romantic music on in the background, hand in hand, lips touching, creating a beautiful moment that they would forever remember.

The pair woke up with a beautiful breakfast served in bed, feeding each other lovingly. The pair went on a shopping trip to see the London Designer Outlet in Wembley. On the way, Adam stopped to buy the new series 3 Apple Watch he had been saving up for a long time. Cameron had a surprise for Adam, but due to the long wait in the Apple store, Cameron got frustrated and did not speak to Adam. Adam asked Cameron "*if everything was okay. Cameron did not reply.*" Clearly something was not right, and both had an ego issue to not resolve it. They walked to the subway, and upon getting on the train, Cameron still did not speak to Adam, which made Adam angry, so he decided to get on a different carriage. Amid the crowd, it was untellable where both Adam and Cameron had got off, causing both to depart from each other. Adam looked for his way, asking strangers. While, on the other hand, Cameron looked for Adam, both searching for each other. With Adam's battery dying, and both unable to reach each other as the network was having a problem, Adam ended up getting out of the station and headed toward a café. Seconds later, Adam received multiple texts stating how much Cameron hated him and never wanted to talk to him ever again. On seeing this, Adam's eyes started filling with tears. Adam called Cameron, not knowing where he was. A stranger came on the phone and told Cameron the location where Adam was. The pair decided to meet halfway; however, Adam was being followed since a long time as he had the series 3 Apple Watch on his back hanging. He reached the station where Cameron was and said "*run*" as he did not want to get any of them in a mess. Cameron applauded Adam for his acting and mocked him for being followed, even though Adam was a stranger in London, and had never been on the public transport before as he always travelled with Cameron in the car. Like this, the pair got in the car and were driving back to London. Adam pulled a pack of chewing gum out: *Big Red*, they were Cameron's favorite.

Cameron: "*Now where did you get these from?*"

Adam: "*From the shop next to the café when I got lost.*"

Cameron: "*Don't lie! You did not get lost; it's all a drama.*"

Adam: "*I love you. Nothing is a drama. I genuinely got lost.*"

Cameron: "*How can you get lost? It's London, anyone can help.*"

Adam: "*Anyone can help, but not when you don't know where you're going yourself and where you got off from. How am I supposed to know where to find you with my battery dying? I panicked! I don't know my way around London.*"

Cameron: "*Look, I've had enough of your drama. I just want to end.*"

Adam: (Crying profusely) "*You really want to end it with me?*"

Cameron: (Angry) "*Yeah, it's over.*"

The couple did not speak to each other all the way home. Adam was in tears while Cameron was full of anger. They both reached their home city when Cameron parked up in the McDonald's car park and both cried their eyes out. The car windows were all steamed up, engine running, sad music playing; both hugging and telling each other how they've had a great time with each other with Cameron ending the relationship there and then.

It was Christmas Eve. Adam was working in the afternoon; Cameron was traveling to London for a week to see his family when he arrived at the store with a letter. Pulling Adam to the side, he said, "*Once I'm gone, read this.*" Adam read the letter, which mentioned "*how Cameron had no one in this city and wanted to give this relationship another chance*" as he was all alone. Adam messaged Cameron: "*I'm ready to give this relationship another chance, but the way I was treated yesterday was unfair. I acknowledge I shouldn't have gone on the other carriage, but you shouldn't have left me. You ended it and I will go by your decision; however, I am no puppet. You ended it with me and then want me. I know I shout, but that's because circumstances bought us to such a stage where you lied to me about many things and cheated me.*"

Cameron was alone in this city as he had no one here except for Adam. However, Adam had been hurt a lot. He was told lies at the start of the relationship. He went for a shoot while his boyfriend was flirting with his makeup artist. He didn't spend any time with Layla to the point he never got intimate with her when he used to meet her. Cameron once asked Adam whom he would choose among the two of them. Adam was quiet. This was the answer that he would choose: Cameron.

One night, Adam was in bed at home wondering to himself, *What is going on? Why am I with someone who is hurting me? Why do I love him so much? He called me at 2 a.m., saying his car broke down, and I went to help him. He called me when he was on the way to London and told me his tires went flat. Why did I go fifty miles to give him tires that he could've gotten? Just because I wanted him to save money? But why do I care so much for him? I ask him for time, which he does give, but why is it I'm ready to do everything for him? He doesn't want me to talk to my friends; I don't. He doesn't even reply to me when he's with his mates, and ignores me! He doesn't want me to do certain things; I don't. I don't understand what's happening to me.?*

CHAPTER 10

Stubbornness Takes Over

Cameron had left for London—streets full of people, roads with traffic, no space to move in the city. Everyone just rushed out partying and enjoying the festive season. During this joyful time, there was a date which was really saddening for Cameron. The date his mum had died: *27th of December.* Due to Cameron being in London, there was no one to go to Cameron's mums grave to pray. In Islam, people pray for the dead; this can be done by reading the Holy Quran or by raising the hands and praying to God.

Adam spoke to Cameron over the phone on Christmas Day.

Adam: "*You had once asked me to go with you to your mum's grave. Are you coming back to visit it for her death anniversary?*"

Cameron: "*No! I'm helping my family move from their house in London.*"

Adam: "*Don't worry! Your mum is like my mum. Give me her full name and graveyard location. I will go pray and place flowers on her grave.*"

Cameron: "*If you're so keen to do so, then go and find it without any details. You have the date and the city she was buried in.*"

Adam: "*Okay! Two days left till her anniversary, and I promise I will find the graveyard and pray for her.*"

Adam spent two days in another city, looking for this one grave. He searched six graveyards, over two thousand graves. He was sick but did not let health get to him as he wanted to pray for her. He kept searching; it was getting dark, no longer safe for him to be in the graveyard. Nevertheless, Adam came across a grave with the same date and just had an inkling this was the one. He called Cameron, but no answer came! He planted flowers and prayed for her. He sent a picture to Cameron to confirm and left.

Moments after, Cameron called and was speechless.

Cameron: "*I'm so sorry I put you through that. I love you and thank you!*"

Adam: "*I wanted you to see her grave through Skype so you'd also pray, but you didn't answer.*"

Cameron: "*It's fine. I prayed from here. Thanks once again!*"

Adam: "*No need for thanks. Like I said, your mum is like mine.*"

Adam had just completely fallen for Cameron; however, it was not the same from both sides as Cameron never truly showed any feelings. In fact, Cameron would doubt Adam for being in his life, like Adam had some reason and at times said.

Cameron: "*I feel like you've come into my life to take something. I mean, no one has ever loved me so much like you have. Why are you here?*"

Adam: "*Don't worry! I don't need anything from you. I'm happy with my life and with what I have. I just love you and can do anything for you!*"

This just shows what love is. It can make people do the craziest things. Love changes a person and their life, both mentally and physically.

Adam visited Cameron in London, exactly a week after the birthday weekend. This time, Adam planned everything and wanted to surprise Cameron. It was mainly an apology for the way the birthday weekend ended. Adam went to London and surprised Cameron, who was shocked but happy. The pair got lunch together and offered Jumah prayer together (a prayer every Muslim offers weekly). The couple went to Winter Wonderland and enjoyed the scariest rides available. Not only that; both the men went to cinema and watched an Arab movie, giving the night a perfect ending with a drive through Oxford Street. During this romantic drive, Adam broke the news of their next adventure, which was to be Amsterdam—Adam's New Year gift to Cameron.

Cameron: "*My uncle said I can't spend any more money as I need to save up for my sister's wedding. Plus, I can't post anything on social media as uncle will know, so what's the point in going?*"

Adam: "*I've booked it now! It's your choice if you want to go! Give me a sec. You're not a baby anymore. You can post wherever you want. You're going on holiday, not doing a crime!*"

Cameron: "*Yeah, but uncle will get suspicious why I am going on holiday with just a guy.*"

Adam: "*Just say it's your mate! I'll be waiting for you at the first location (where the couple had met).*"

Cameron: "*I'll see if I can come.*"

Adam just couldn't understand. Cameron was grown enough to move cities for his job, then why does he have to ask his uncle about going on holiday with his friends? It seemed a bit dodgy. It's not like he must tell his uncle.

CHAPTER 11

Amsterdam

The New Year's resolution for the couple was to argue less. Adam was ill but faked a smile. He did not want anyone to know he was getting ill. As Adam had said, he would be waiting at the first location for Cameron. A car arrived; it was Cameron. That's where both men met up and left for the airport.

They got the flight from London to Amsterdam. However, on the flight, the couple argued, Cameron lied again. On landing in Amsterdam, Cameron didn't appear in front of Adam and he, like a crazy person, went looking for him, making announcements. He searched every carousel, men's toilets, not knowing where Cameron was.

On the other hand, Cameron sat at a Burger King, playing this mind game with Adam, leaving him to search for him was disgraceful. Adam was worried mad, running up and down the airport. Finally, Cameron called Adam.

Cameron: "*Why are you worrying for me? Stop running up and down the airport. I will make my own way to the hotel.*"

Adam: "*Just stop it and come in front of me.*"

Cameron came in front of Adam. Both walked to the kiosk to get train passes. Adam was angry that he vented his anger out there and then. He started arguing with Cameron in front of everyone. Cameron retaliated and made comments to make Adam even angrier after a stressful situation he had put him in. Cameron went left and Adam went right. They went their own ways.

Adam reached the hotel. Cameron was standing in the reception area. He couldn't check in without Adam as the booking was under his name. Adam had the room decorated. Even after the argument, he took Cameron to the room and surprised him.

Cameron walked inside. Rose petals all over the floor led toward the bed, which had a heart made, and the room was full of rose petals. Mood lights were on, slow music played. Adam invited him inside. The couple just hugged and made out like there was no tomorrow. *But who knew this holiday would once again be another victim of a breakup?* During this holiday, the couple had many arguments and left each other at times for petty little reasons. Cameron had played another mind game with Adam. The holiday ended with both going back to London not talking to each other, and once again Cameron had ended it with Adam. Cameron messaged Adam's friend Alex regarding this and was advised to "*Let it go.*"

The New Year's resolution the couple had made was clearly not going to plan. Once again, the lovers had split up and it was Cameron who had broken up this time as well.

CHAPTER 12

The Cheat

A few days had passed by. The couple were arguing on Snapchat, both bringing up the past, not accepting their mistakes, just arguing. With this, the misunderstanding just grew, but Adam called Cameron to his workplace after he had finished work to talk. The guys met and went for a late night meal, where they spoke and resolved why Cameron was behaving like this. At this point, Adam was so attached to Cameron, he wouldn't let go and would apologize even if it was not his mistake at times. He grew much closer to Cameron and went further apart from Layla. He didn't spend any time with her at all. He would make excuses and meet Cameron.

Moreover, time was going so fast, days were passing by, weeks were flying, and soon came Cameron's sister's wedding time. Cameron had to fl y abroad. The wedding was taking place in Yemen, but Cameron wanted to travel by a connecting flight to Qatar and stay over for two days. Adam offered to get a flight to Qatar while he would be there for two days and they could spend time together as Cameron would be alone and would get bored. *Who knew this was all a big plan?* A setup. Cameron made excuses: "*I might not go. If I do go, my brother said he wants to go.*" Adam kept quiet and let Cameron do what he wanted.

Cameron was in Yemen and was talking to Adam the first couple of days. Adam was to go to the wedding, but Cameron's uncle didn't allow any friends to come as Cameron told Adam. It was Valentines day, *14th of February*. Since Adam was not allowed to attend the wedding, he sent the dance video via WhatsApp to Cameron. He was learning for the wedding. Cameron spoke to Adam for the last time here. Five days later, Cameron reached Qatar alone. Cameron had been ignoring all of Adam's text messages for five days and declining his calls, even though he was actively posting on social media. Adam was starstruck!

Upon arriving in Qatar, Cameron called Adam for the first time in five days.

Cameron: "*How's it going?*"

Adam: "*It's going good. How come you didn't talk to me for the past five days?*"

Cameron: "*My aunty had seen my phone and our nude pictures together.*"

Adam: "*Oh god! But one text you could've sent…it was not like she was with you when you went to the toilet.*"

Cameron: "*Yeah, I could've, but I didn't want her to know I was talking to you!*"

Adam: "*But you were posting! You could've just sent a text saying this!*"

The guys spoke, but what Cameron didn't know, Adam got one of his friend Billy to talk to Cameron whilst he was not talking to Adam for the five days on holiday. However, Cameron was talking to other guys on Facebook but not to Adam.

Adam let it go and sent some attractions to Cameron, so he could see and enjoy as Cameron went alone to Qatar and not with family or his brother, which was the other lie he told, as before he left he stated he was going with his family.

The second night was the night that changed everything. The relationship of trust turned into a *one-night stand!* Cameron decided to put Grindr on and slept with a guy in Qatar. After sleeping with someone in Qatar, he sent a snap to Adam. The snap was a box of chocolates in a heart shape, stating: *Happy five months, sweetheart!*

Adam was unaware of what Cameron had done. He had full trust in Cameron, never mind him doing such a low act, he didn't imagine Cameron speaking to a guy in any way more than friends.

CHAPTER 13

Unfolding Truth

Cameron was heading back to London from Qatar, where he had committed this act of cheating. He did not tell Adam anything.

Full of happiness, Adam got a bus to Heathrow Airport, not booking a return ticket, even though he had a flight in eight hours' time from Manchester. He arrived, all excited to see his boyfriend. But Cameron was angry upon seeing Adam. They drove back, and Cameron kept everything hidden and snogged Adam. He gave him a gift he had gotten from Qatar for him. Adam said, "*I have not come here for a gift; I have come here because I missed you so much. It's been ages since I saw you, and I have a flight in a few hours, which means I won't see you for a long week.*" The couple hugged as though everything was okay, but only Cameron knew what he had done in Qatar. Adam left for his flight.

A few days into his holiday in Europe, Adam was asked by Cameron to call him right away. Adam went to the lobby of the hotel and called right away. The couple did a video call. Cameron was really upset. He was nervous. He was behaving unusually.

Adam: "*What's up? Is everything okay?*"

Cameron: "*What would break us up? What's the most disgusting act I can do to hurt you?*"

Adam: "*The day you cheat me, that's the day we break up!*"

(Cameron cries louder. Tears flow down his eyes, he is unable to speak.)

Adam: "*Have you cheated on me?*" His heart beats faster.

Cameron: "*Yeah.*"

Adam shaking, tears rolling down his eyes. He was not able to say anything. Things get heated up. Cameron crying on the other line. Adam is not able to think how this even happened.

Adam: "*How? In Yemen?*"

Cameron: "*No, Qatar. I'm so sorry.*"

The phone dropped from Adam's hands and Adam couldn't stop crying. The hotel staff worried what went off so suddenly. Other tourists in the hotel wondered if Adam was okay. All that could be heard was Adam's heartbeat that was loud and thumping as this news just destroyed Adam. He could not think of anything. It was so painful. Adam felt like someone had destroyed his whole life. It was a pain that no one could understand.

CHAPTER 14

Contemplation Time

Adam's holiday was destroyed. He couldn't think of anything. He just wanted to be away from everyone. He booked camping for two days to another city in Morocco—a quiet place, where he could just spend time alone. He contemplated. He knew what he was doing all this time was love. He also knew it was not accepted due to their religion; however, he still carried the relationship, distancing himself away from Layla, who was his fiancée.

While on this two-day trip away from all, Adam realised Cameron did not love him; it was all lust. If it was really love, he wouldn't ever have done this to him.

Adam was so upset and confined himself. He did not speak to anyone throughout his holiday. The holiday was no longer anything to enjoy. Adam's family started getting worried as to why Adam went quiet suddenly. This whole situation got to Adam so much, it made him ill. Adam was admitted to hospital. His health had had deteriorated.

Not long was left until it was time for Adam to come back to the United Kingdom. He was accompanied by the medical team on the flight that assisted him throughout his history of being terminal, and they did not want to risk anything. Adam was scared. He did not want to come back as he would break down more.

CHAPTER 15

The Confrontation

Thomas Cook's flight had landed in the UK. As soon as it landed, Cameron called Adam, but he did not answer. He did not want to speak to anyone. He was distraught. It was Thursday midnight. Roads to and from the airport were cordoned off due to the Snow. Cameron had booked a hotel for Adam to stay nearby as he could not reach home until the morning at the very earliest. Adam's driver came and picked him up. Spending the night in the car on the motorway, Adam and his family did not reach home until 10 a.m. on Friday morning. Adam left for university and from there he went to Friday prayers where he encountered Cameron.

He did not want to speak to him, but purposely Cameron made a conversation and the couple agreed to meet in the evening to have a chat.

The pair met after a few hours. They stayed in a hotel, spoke and Cameron deliberately had sex with Adam. *But before this, they spoke about who did wrong and how to move forward from this.* Cameron kept asking for forgiveness regarding the shameful act he had committed. Adam couldn't see him cry and saw him repent, so he forgave him, even after Adam's friends said not to.

The couple gave their relationship a new start. Adam did forgive but could not forget this big cheat. Adam was depressed. He stopped taking care of himself. He didn't want to get ready anymore. No one could feel what he was feeling. As weeks passed by, Cameron and Adam would meet but it wasn't the same. Adam would be suspicious about many things. Cameron started saying, "*What we were doing was wrong by religion, so me doing what I did in Qatar isn't anything worse.*" Adam was stunned. Cameron didn't feel true repentance. Adam felt used as he gave everything to Cameron. Adam even questioned Cameron. "*What did that man have that I did not? Why did you not just end it with me before doing this?" I gave you everything and most precious was our love. How could you even forget that?*" Cameron had no answer, and as time passed, he didn't feel bad about anything of what he did. Adam's mates knew what was going on between them both, and Cameron was speaking to them telling them to end it with his fiancé or end it with him.

CHAPTER 16

Turkey

Weeks after trying to get over the deceit Cameron had caused Adam, the holiday Adam and his mates had booked to Turkey had finally arrived. The pair had broken up a couple of times, and weeks before Turkey, Cameron kept ending it. Adam thought this was the time to move on, but just could not. His love for Cameron was too deep. *Cameron was causing grief to Adam, accusing him of always wanting this holiday to have sex with other guys.*

Adam and his friend left for Turkey and while there, Adam would picture himself with Cameron and no one else. Moving on was a far step; he could not speak to another guy in that manner.

On return from his holiday, Cameron met Adam. He knew Adam did not meet anyone but still wanted to have an argument.

Cameron: "*Did you enjoy guys Turkey?*"

Adam: "*What do you think?*"

Cameron did not answer as he knew Adam could not move on. Cameron would manipulate a lot and never admit he's wrong in anything. It's his way or no one's way. Despite Cameron cheating, he would check Adam's phone, input his password, and know who Adam's friends are. Even after being cheated on, Adam never checked

Cameron's phone. Not only this; *Cameron accused Adam of having him for a sidechick and was using him for his sexual desires. Cameron wanted Adam to tell his family everything about them. Adam wondered whether he'd been cheated on before and if this was the right move to make.*

CHAPTER 17

Truth Came Out

Adam was heading out for university when Cameron had sent a snap to Adam. Layla saw the expressions on Adam's face when seeing this snap. She saw Adam's messages with Cameron and questioned him.

Layla: "*What's all this?*"

Adam: "*Nothing. It's just Cameron is having a breakup situation with his girlfriend and I'm helping him solve the situation.*"

Layla: "*And this so-called GF slept with men in Turkey and got a scholarship in France and is going to have sexual intercourse with other guys?*"

Adam: "*Yeah! We've been talking in the sense how he would be talking to his girl-friend; hence, we gave it real-life scenarios.*"

Adam convinced her and she believed him. On the way to university, Adam was thinking of the conversation he had at times with Cameron on how he felt he was being used as a "*side-chick.*" Adam managed to cover up this time, but he was not completely satisfied as he wanted to make his boyfriend happy. He met Cameron on his lunchbreak. Cameron advised him "*to go back to his family and forget them both ever had anything.*" Adam saw Cameron's behaviour. So Adam called his mum, uncle, and sister to the local café.

Adam was really nervous, he was shaking. His throat was really dry, and he was trying not to break down. He decided to reveal today. He said it!

Adam: "*I'm gay. I love Cameron.*"

Everyone: *"What?"*

Adam's uncle: "*Are you having a laugh?*"

Adam's mum: "*You have a fiancée?*"

Adam: "*Yeah, but I cannot betray her anymore and I want to be with this guy.*"

Adam's sister: "*You're getting married soon. Have you lost it?*"

Adam: "*I don't know. I want to settle down with him. I know being a Muslim this is impossible, but this is what I want and he said he will support me.*"

Adam's mum: "*I'll support you. I'm there for you. The question is, does he love you also? And will he tell his family about you?*"

Adam knew Cameron would support him and would not leave him. Adam was relieved he had told his family. He did this for Cameron. Adam would've never fallen for a guy, but he did, and this man changed him. He did something he never thought of and told his family, even after being betrayed by Cameron.

Both the men met that weekend and went to Manchester together. During this trip, Cameron had shown his true colours. Adam told Cameron everything and how his mum said, "*She'll support them.*" On hearing this, Cameron was annoyed. He abandoned Adam and did not contact him again. He gave their relationship a finish. He left without thinking how Adam would've felt.

Days passed by. Adam was alone. He would commute to university and not talk to anyone. He would come back and lock himself up in the room. He did not shave for days; he did not feel like doing anything. His life had changed from bringing a smile to everyone's face to forcing himself to smile. He had been betrayed once again. He did everything he could for Cameron. Whatever Cameron wanted, he would do. Regardless of the consequences, he would do it, because he knew this would make Cameron happy. Adam had an exam in the next twenty-four hours. He did not revise at all for it. He did not have the motivation to study anymore. He did not want to do anything. He would listen to music and cry in bed. He would not sleep at night. Even the tissues were tired of wiping Adam's tears.

Living in today's society, people think two men cannot share a bond together. Religion does not define or stop any individual. In the Holy Quran, it does not mention anything about homosexuality directly. The Islamic condemnation of homosexuality, people believe, is based directly on the Quranic story of Prophet Lut, known as Lot in the Christian context. This story is repeated a few times in different verses, following a similar form. This story of Prophet Lut, his family, and the destruction of Sodom and Gomorrah is mentioned in many verses: 7:80, 11:77, 15:59, 21:71, 26:161, 27:55, 29:26, 37:133 and 54:33. Coming to the lecherous act and the history of this story reveals both the cities were destroyed with fire and brimstones. Philo of Alexandria interprets this centuries later, along with other religious writers, to have been the rage of god's penalty for the homosexuality of people. According to many modern-day scholars, it is likely that the story of Sodom and Gomorrah may not involve homosexuality at all. People have interpreted it to be this over time; however, no verse in the Holy Quran directly quotes homosexuality. Furthermore, for the sake of argument, even if this is believed, the condemnation of homosexuality based on the Holy Quran—and people are still committing this—in the eyes of God is regarded as a sin. God forgives every sin, except those sins that use his name in vain. Religion cannot be blamed as Islam is a religion that is peaceful and promotes a balanced way of life.

CHAPTER 18

Finally Moved On

Everything for Adam was over. He had no one by his side. He felt like this was it. Cameron, who was the love of his life had left him, nor did he have Layla by his side.

Adam decided to leave the country and start anew. He couldn't take it, being in the same country as Cameron, where he would be constantly hurt. Adam got a job in Dubai and had moved over. Before leaving the country, Adam dropped a letter to Cameron's workplace. It was the last one. Adam arrived at the airport and following him came Cameron. It was too late. Adam had checked in, ready to leave the country. Cameron tried to convince Adam to stay, but Adam's heart was too wounded to stay. He had lost everyone; his life had completely changed. He took this decision after thinking a lot about Cameron. Adam explained everything, how the guy he had come out to regarding his sexuality was the one who ditched him. Adam left, leaving everything behind and moving to Dubai. This was the first time he had moved on physically.

Time was passing by in Dubai. Adam was living his new life differently and exploring the country, till he was hit by aching discomfort and had to be admitted in hospital. All of a sudden, Adam got sick! He had to catch the next flight back to the UK for treatment.

His doctor had everything organized. He did not tell anyone and came back. His body was not responding to any treatment.

Cameron met Adam. He said, "*I know what you did in Dubai and I forgive you. I know you still love me, yet I am willing to forget everything and let's move in together.*"

Adam: "*I know I still love you, but coming back to you means I have no self-respect. You had left me even after everything I did for us. I'm sorry! You cheated me and then betrayed me. I forgave you after what you did in Qatar, but not now! You betrayed me multiple times.*"

Cameron repeatedly accusing Adam and saying unusual stuff to him.

Cameron: "*Hope you enjoyed it in Dubai with other guys.*"

Adam: "*Yes, I did. And I moved on. It took me three months, but it was after you decided to sleep in bed with another man and betrayed me so many times.*"

Cameron was being despicable. On the other hand, Adam had to shift back to the UK. He was terminal. He wanted to be away from the UK but could not be too far. In case anything happened, he could easily get medical attention, so he decided to complete a semester in France.

Amid all this, Cameron and Adam would meet, as Cameron deliberately kept stalking Adam, not letting him live his life and move on. Cameron attended all the same events as Adam. He met Adam in the supermarket and in the shopping mall. Both were not in communication with each other but Cameron kept stalking Adam and had a tracker on his car; knowing wherever Adam was going. On the day when the pair met at the shopping mall, Adam saw Cameron texting a guy.

Adam: "*Is everything okay?*"

Cameron: "*Yeah. We were just talking about our holiday.*"

Adam: "*I thought you were going on holiday with your old university mates? Weren't there like three guys and two girls going?*"

Cameron: "*No, I'm going with Roy and Sophie.*"

Adam: "*Do you really think Sophie's parents will let her go with two guys, like really? Remember where we hail from, Yemen.*"

Cameron: "*Yeah, she's not going. Only Roy and I are!*"

Adam: "*Really? But isn't he the same guy you said that asked you to go on holiday with alone and you said he likes you?*"

Cameron: "*Yeah, he's the same guy, but we're just brothers!*"

Adam: "*Cut the crap, brothers! Please them, me, and you are also brothers! You are going to go on holiday with a guy who has feelings for you and sleep on a double bed with him. I just can't believe it. Why do you want to reconcile with me then? Like, clearly you going to hurt me.*"

Cameron: "*You're overreacting. He's my brother.*"

Adam: "*Okay. Don't go on holiday with him!*"

Cameron: "*I'm going on holiday with him. No one can stop us.*"

Both could not be away from each other, however much they wanted to. Their relationship was something no one had witnessed before. It was full of love and happiness from Adam, but loads of pain and cheat given from Cameron. Adam was to leave for France for a long four months. Bearing in mind the critical situation between both the men, they had their relationship on a hope. *'Neither of them slept with anyone in the next four months.'* Adam was determined to pass this love test but was worried if Cameron would be able to. Cameron gave his word, "*I promise, even if you sleep with anyone or move on, I will still complete the four months until you're back.*"

The summer had started, Adam was in Paris, also known as the city of love! Days had gone by, weeks had passed, the men were not in touch, blocking and unblocking each other on social media, stalking each other but not greeting one another. Until, one day, Adam decided to test Cameron to see if he was actually worth spending his whole life with after the problems in the past.

Adam: (Typing) "*Hey, I've moved on.*"

Cameron: (Shocked) "*What? How could you? You promised four months? Swear on my mum, and I know you won't swear by my mum falsely.*"

Adam: "*Nope. I won't swear by her. But this is what I've done. Are you going to move on now?*"

Cameron: (Tears coming down his face) "*No! I'm not like you. I will keep my promise and still won't sleep with anyone for the remaining couple of months. I promised, and I will keep it. I'm blocking you. You don't deserve me.*"

Adam was happy to hear this. He wrote a postcard with first class delivery stating the truth. It was posted and delivered the very next day. Regardless, Cameron ignored that and made a new online account. Billy sent a screenshot to Adam showing him how Cameron was meeting other men. Cameron had broken his promise, even after knowing the truth in the postcard. Adam called him many times, sent text messages, got his friend to try stopping Cameron from sleeping with anyone, but he did not pay any heed. He just ignored everything, and within two days of Adam's test, he slept with someone. He failed. For Cameron, it was always just lust and he had proved it. He did not have to sleep with anyone, but chose to, just because he wanted sex all along! Moving on is not having sex with others.

CHAPTER 19

The first shall be the last

Adam had to have surgery in the next two weeks, and it was Cameron's birthday in two days' time. Adam could not leave till after another week, but he came back because he wanted to surprise Cameron and give him a good birthday. He planned everything for it, but Cameron did not agree to go with him. He was being stubborn. Adam faked a smile, just so he could give Cameron a good time for a few days while he was in the country. This is why Adam flew back so early.

Cameron: "*This is part of your plan!*"

Adam: "*I'm here for you! I don't want sex. I just want to give you a few days of smile.*"

Cameron: "*I don't trust you, after you've been to France and sleeping with other guys like you said. It was true, wasn't it? It was no test!*"

Adam: "*It was a test, but believe what you can. For now, let's forget the past and enjoy!*"

Throughout the few days the pair spent together, they had spoken a lot, and Cameron admitted going to Switzerland with Roy, the male who had feelings for Cameron. Throughout Adam and Cameron's relationship, Roy and Cameron were in touch. Cameron classified this as a "*brotherhood relationship*."

Cameron was treating Adam badly, taunting him, making him feel guilty. Adam tolerated it for so long, but just couldn't anymore and came out with everything—why he did what he did and how Cameron had failed the test.

Cameron got his answers but did not have any regret. He had failed to save his love, but blamed Adam for everything saying he was a cheater and forced him to sleep with someone. It takes two to tango; it was simply Cameron's choice to sleep with another man. Both went their own ways. Cameron messaged Adam "*never to come in front of him again*."

As time passed, Adam was recovering from his illness. Cameron was busy in his life. Adam missed Cameron so much, but remembered what was told to him. He went lowkey. He did not face Cameron, instead he was getting messages and calls from unknown people who were asked by Cameron to contact and harass Adam to make him feel guilty. They said to him he faked his illness and also told him about the time he had left. When Adam went to France, he was told he had only "*three months left to live*." This was only told to Cameron when he was being accused continuously, but Cameron believed this to be a lie also as Adam had a turnover and was surviving beyond the time given by medics. It's not in the doctor's hands to give a verdict about someone's life time; however, they give a rough idea. Nevertheless, Cameron's plan was working; Adam was so depressed and was losing his self-confi dence. He was being emotionally and mentally blackmailed. Cameron said before and again about leaving the city as this city had given him not just "*love*" but more "*pain, cheating, and lies*."

After all, what was it that Cameron wanted? *Why didn't he let Adam be in peace*? Many times, Cameron had broken their relationship. He tested Adam throughout their time together, and every time Adam passed to the extent that Adam came out to his family for him. Cameron promised he would be there for him but was not.

Cameron was a genuine guy who cared a lot about people but was not suitable for a relationship. He could not commit, even after someone doing so much for him. In the same manner, Adam gave his all to Cameron but got betrayed continuously. Adam would lose his temper because of this, but they say, "*You argue with those you love.*" The negative aspect about Adam was he would keep everything in and not tell anyone the pain he would experience. He felt Cameron was the right person in such a short span of time. He wronged Layla as he kept her in the dark, hence the same happened to him: karma! What goes around comes around! Whenever Adam would see Layla, his eyes would dwell with tears as he knew how much he had wronged her.

Knowing he was from a religion where people would not accept their relationship, both the men decided to do this—they carried on. Cameron cheated Adam even after knowing he had a fiancée but loved him. Cameron also knew Adam did not have sex with Layla since both men had met. Adam disclosed everything. Adam still decided to be with Cameron, even after the deceit he received. *Was this not true love*?

Love is a struggle, and once you have attained that struggle, it isn't recognised as love. That love fades away once you have it with you. It is a desire that you care for. People call this "*love,*" but it is care you maintain, and that's what Adam was receiving from Cameron. It was Cameron's guilt that made him reveal his demeaning act that had created all these problems. If Cameron was sincere from the start and didn't do the same that had happened to him as he stated—which was his ex-boyfriend cheating with him—then today life would've been different. Adam thought for months Cameron was truly his. He thought he was living a new life, found tranquillity, love, and peaceful serenity, despite knowing he was terminal and time was against him. Weaker than before, Adam showed great strength, doing all those activities that others would by trying to match Cameron's spirit as he did not want Cameron to stop doing activities he couldn't; for example, trying to get a six-pack in the gym so Cameron would be impressed, even after knowing he couldn't due to health issues. The unconditional love Adam gave was never given to anyone else. The love that Cameron had for

Adam was not love but always claimed it to be. Adam tried his best to move on; however, Cameron wouldn't let him and would do something new to contact him or appear in front of him. Cameron harassed Adam from time to time and tracked all his steps. He made fake accounts and spoke to him portraying to be someone else.

As time passed, Adam met Cameron. He decided to speak to Cameron regarding either sorting everything out or to put an end to it right away. Adam gave Cameron the same white chocolates he gave him the very first day they had become official. Adam went to Cameron's office and waited for over forty-five minutes. Cameron came out and rebuked Adam to wait elsewhere. So, he did. They met. Cameron spoke and Adam listened for four hours. Cameron vented out all his frustration and anger toward him. He was hurting Adam more, but Adam kept quiet and agreed with everything.

Cameron: "*Your love was always fake! Everything you said, did, felt—nothing was real.*"

Adam: (Smiling) "*Hmmm.*"

Cameron: "*You are a cheater, liar, fake. You lied about your health, love, feelings. It was just an experience for you! You're the worst thing that ever happened to me!*"

Adam: (Controlling his tears) *"Hmmm."*

Cameron: "*I'm leaving this city because of you. I'm tired of fake people and this fake city.*" This was the second time Cameron had said this but never left the city.

Cameron was constantly swaying his anger on Adam and blaming him for everything while he was quietly listening. Not uttering a word, controlling his tears, and holding a brave face, Adam just smiled.

Adam: "*You can't clap with one hand, it takes two! I'm sorry for everything; you're right. I am a fake, unreal, a cheat. Anything else you want to say?*"

Cameron: "*Why are you here?*"

Adam: "*I had come here with the same white chocolates as the first official date. I had come here to reconcile; however, that cannot happen. They say whatever happens, it happens for a reason. My coming here today was good, at least I found out the hate you have for me!*"

Cameron: "*You're fake, just fake!*"

Adam: "*I take everything on me. It was all my fault. Just be happy and enjoy your life and the new city you move to. I just hope you don't meet anyone so disgusting like me.*"

Cameron: "*I'm so naive, but I've learned a lot from you. I've learned how to do anal when I wasn't used to committing such an act. Don't worry, I won't meet anyone like you because you're just the only one who is so cheap.*"

The pair ended their meet and walked away. It was devastating! Two people who loved each other so much...but something was stopping them from being together.

One thing that was not told throughout the whole year was Cameron cheated Adam all this time with a guy he had said at the start of the relationship was his ex. Cameron admitted it to Adam a few days before his birthday. It was a big game, but at the same time Cameron would not leave Adam. It was a charm Adam had that no one had.

At times, when individuals walk away from your life, let them go. Your fate is never tied to anyone who leaves you, and it doesn't mean they are bad people; it simply means that their part in your story is over. After all, what was this breathtaking relationship Adam and Cameron experienced?

If you have anything you would like to feedback to Adnan, regarding the book or how you feel, please feel free to email him on: adnan.hussain123@hotmail.co.uk

CPSIA information can be obtained
at www.ICGtesting.com
Printed in the USA
BVHW030859071119
563170BV00001B/104/P

9 781643 486598